A Note to Parents

DK READERS is a compelling programme for beginning readers, designed in conjunction with leading literacy experts, including Maureen Fernandes, B.Ed (Hons). Maureen has spent many years teaching literacy, both in the classroom and as a consultant in schools.

Beautiful illustrations and superb full-colour photographs combine with engaging, easy-to-read stories to offer a fresh approach to each subject in the series. Each DK READER is guaranteed to capture a child's interest while developing his or her reading skills, general knowledge, and love of reading.

The five levels of DK READERS are aimed at different reading abilities, enabling you to choose the books that are exactly right for your child:

Pre-level 1: Learning to read
Level 1: Beginning to read
Level 2: Beginning to read alone
Level 3: Reading alone
Level 4: Proficient readers

The "normal" age at which a child begins to read can be anywhere from three to eight years old. Adult participation through the lower levels is very helpful for providing encouragement, discussing storylines, and sounding out unfamiliar words.

No matter which level you select, you can be sure that you are helping your child learn to read, then read to learn!

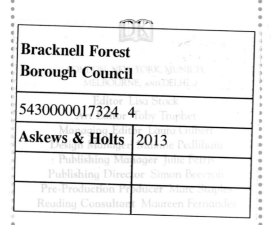

LONDON, NEW YORK, MUNICH,
MELBOURNE, and DELHI

Editor Lisa Stock
Designer Toby Truphet
Managing Editor Laura Gilbert
Design Manager Maxine Pedliham
Publishing Manager Julie Ferris
Publishing Director Simon Beecroft
Pre-Production Producer Marc Staples
Reading Consultant Maureen Fernandes

DK India
Editor Rahul Ganguly
Senior Editor Garima Sharma
Assistant Art Editors Karan Chaudhary,
Chitrak Srivastava
Deputy Managing Art Editor Neha Ahuja
Pre-Production Manager Sunil Sharma
DTP Designer Manish Upreti

For Lucasfilm
Executive Editor J.W. Rinzler
Art Director Troy Alders
Keeper of the Holocron Leland Chee
Director of Publishing Carol Roeder

First published in Great Britain in 2013 by
Dorling Kindersley Limited,
80 Strand, London, WC2R 0RL

13 14 15 16 10 9 8 7 6 5 4 3 2 1
001-187420-Nov/13

A CIP record for this book is available
from the British Library.

ISBN: 978-1-40932-547-5

Colour reproduction by Altaimage, UK
Printed and bound by L-Rex Printing Co., Ltd, China

Discover more at
www.dk.com
www.starwars.com

Contents

DK READERS

BEGINNING 1 TO READ

ARE EWOKS SCARED OF STORMTROOPERS?

Written by Catherine Saunders

Unlikely heroes

Being big and strong does not mean you will win every battle.

Heroes can come in all shapes and sizes.

Jar Jar
Binks

Anakin
Skywalker

Wicket

Sometimes it is the ones you least expect who save the day.

As Master Yoda wisely says, "Size matters not".

R2-D2

Master Yoda

Furry warriors

These stormtroopers are following evil orders on the forest moon of Endor.

The small, furry Ewoks who live there have no armour or blasters … but they aren't scared of the stormtroopers!

The brave Ewoks fight with stones and spears to save their forest home.

7

Daring rebel

The Death Star is a huge weapon with the power to destroy a whole planet.

Can young rebel pilot Luke Skywalker defeat a weapon the size of a small moon?

Yes! He flies his X-wing right up to the Death Star and destroys it with a well-aimed blast!

X-wing

Battling Binks

Watch out! These battle droids are armed.

Battle droids

Sometimes a clumsy general can actually be a help in battle!

Jar Jar Binks

Energy ball

Jar Jar Binks accidentally releases some energy balls.

Smash! A whole group of battle droids is wiped out.

Droid
Control Ship

Child's play

Anakin Skywalker is only
nine years old, but he is a very
brave pilot.

Anakin

Starfighter

In a space battle, little Anakin flies his starfighter inside the Droid Control Ship undetected.

He hits just the spot to destroy the ship and win the battle!

Dinner time

This hungry rancor is looking for his next meal.

He wants it to be the Jedi Luke Skywalker!

Sharp claws

The rancor may be bigger,
but Luke is much cleverer.

Luke traps the scary beast
and escapes to safety.

Princess in peril

Jabba the Hutt is a crime lord. He takes Princess Leia prisoner as his slave.

It looks like she will never escape!

Princess Leia

The princess patiently waits until Jabba is distracted.

Then Leia uses her chains to defeat the huge Hutt.

Jabba

Working together

Jedi Obi-Wan Kenobi is about to be eaten by a fierce acklay.

Obi-Wan cannot escape his wild opponent alone.

Jedi

Obi-Wan
Kenobi

Luckily, he isn't alone for long!

Obi-Wan's friends arrive riding on a reek, just in time to carry him away.

Reek

Acklay

19

AT-AT attack

The AT-ATs are huge walking tanks on legs.

The rebel pilots cannot defeat them by firepower alone.

Snowspeeder

Luckily, the rebels have a brilliant plan.

They trip up the AT-ATs using cables fired from their snowspeeders.

Nimble Jedi

The Sith Lords Darth Sidious and Dooku are very powerful.

Jedi Master Yoda is very powerful, too but he is also very small.

Darth Sidious

Master Yoda

Despite his size, the Jedi jumps and leaps extremely fast.

Even the Sith Lords cannot defeat him in a duel.

Dooku

Clever thinking

A Star Destroyer is chasing
a rebel ship called the
Millennium Falcon.

Rebel pilot Han Solo tries to
lose the huge Star Destroyer by
leading it into an asteroid field.

Han Solo

Han knows that his small ship can dart between the space rocks, but the Star Destroyer is much too big to do that!

Millennium Falcon

Star Destroyer

Droid vs droid

A little droid like R2-D2 doesn't scare these big, bad super battle droids.

R2-D2

But they should be scared!

Tiny R2-D2 squirts the super battle droids with oil and then sets them on fire.

Super battle droid

Brave leader

A new, even bigger Death Star has been built!

Han Solo's friend Lando Calrissian is leading a dangerous attack mission.

He flies the *Millennium Falcon* inside the Death Star and helps his team destroy it.

The galaxy is free!

Victory!

Now you have met some of
the galaxy's greatest and least
likely heroes.

They may be younger, weaker or smaller than their enemies, but they have great courage.

Would you be as brave as them?

Glossary

Battle droids
Soldier droids made for fighting.

Jedi
A member of a group that fights evil.

Snowspeeder
A flying vehicle that can travel over snow.

Starfighter
A small spacecraft that can take sharp turns.

X-wing
A one-man spacecraft with excellent weapons.